The Case of
the Flying
Toenails

SECRET AGENT DINGLEDORF

... and his trusty dog, SPLAT

The Case of the Flying Toenails

BILL MYERS

Illustrations
Meredith Johnson

Tommy NELSON®

www.tommynelson.com

A Division of Thomas Nelson, Inc.
www.ThomasNelson.com

Text copyright © 2002 by Bill Myers
Illustrations by Meredith Johnson. Copyright © 2002 by Tommy Nelson®, a Division of Thomas Nelson, Inc.

Published in Nashville, Tennessee, by Tommy Nelson®, a Division of Thomas Nelson, Inc.

Library of Congress Cataloging-in-Publication Data

Myers, Bill, 1953-
  The case of the flying toenails / by Bill Myers.
    p. cm.490—(Secret Agent Dingledorf . . . and his trusty dog, Splat ; 3)
  Summary: Ten-year-old secret agent Bernie Dingledorf tells a lie and helps expose the world to a dreaded cold that makes jets of flame come out through your toenails.
  ISBN: 1-4003-0096-7
  [1. Cold (Disease)—Fiction 2. Spies—Fiction. 3. Honesty—Fiction. 4. Christian life—Fiction. 5. Humorous stories.] I. Title.
PZ7.M98234 Cao 2002
[Fic]—dc21   2002070918

Printed in the United States of America

02 03 04 05 06 PHX 5 4 3 2 1

For Mrs. Delahooke
and her third-grade class

"The LORD detests lying lips, but he delights in men who are truthful."

—Proverbs 12:22 (NIV)

Contents

CHAPTER 1

The Case Begins

The next time I decide to lie, do me a favor. Tell me I'll have to watch *Blue's Clues* nonstop for a month.

Better yet, tell me I'll have to listen to Barney the dinosaur's theme song a million times.

Do whatever it takes to stop me.

Why?

Because I discovered that lying is as much fun as eating cream of spinach soup in the middle of a math test while you've got the chickenpox!

Okay, it's not really that bad.

IT'S WORSE!

(Sorry, didn't mean to yell.)

It all started when Splat, the Wonderdog, and I crawled out onto our roof from my bedroom.

There were a bunch of shooting stars that night, and we wanted to see them.

Mom and Dad had said it was too late.

I always try to obey my folks, but there was something about the stars. There was also something about Priscilla banging on my window and threatening to beat me up if I didn't get out of bed.

(Priscilla knows karate, kung fu, Kung Pao Chicken, and all that stuff.)

We've been next-door neighbors ever since we were kids. We've been friends almost as long. (I know she's a girl, but it's great having someone to protect me from all the sixth-grade bullies.)

I can't remember the last time she used our front door. With a giant tree between our houses and her ability to climb trees, why bother?

So there we were, Priscilla, Splat, and I, lying on our backs, staring up at the stars, when . . .

"AUGHHH . . ."
K-Thud

we were joined by a fourth person (whose tree climbing wasn't quite as good as Priscilla's).

At first, I thought it was my older cousin Wally McDoogle. Wally is always falling out of trees and stuff. If there is such a thing as a walking disaster, it's Wally.

People say Wally and I are nothing alike
. . . especially when it comes to athletic
ability.

I have some.

He has none.

But it wasn't Wally. It was some lady
in a black hat and a trench coat.

Luckily, the roof stopped her fall.
Unluckily, it might have also stopped her
breathing.

"Lady!" I shouted. "Lady, are you all
right?"

Her eyes were closed and she groaned.

Oh, and there was one other thing . . .
her face was glowing green.

HER FACE WAS
GLOWING GREEN!
(Oops, I'm yelling again.

Is this better?)

"Who is she?" Priscilla asked.

There was something about the way the letters B.A.D.D. were written on the back of her coat, on her binoculars, on her pocket, and on her hat, that caused me to make a brilliant guess.

"She might be a B.A.D.D. agent," I said. (I told you it was brilliant.) "You know, **B**ungling **A**gents **D**edicated to **D**estruction."

Priscilla turned to me. "Those are the bad guys who think you're a secret agent?" she asked.

I nodded.

"So what was she doing?"

"Probably spying on me."

"But why is she glowing green?"

Before we had an answer, the agent . . .

"*AH-CHOOO!*"-ed

into all three of our faces.

"Gross," Priscilla groaned as we all wiped off the wetness. (Some people pass out towels when they sneeze. This woman should have passed out raincoats.)

But that was just the beginning. Because suddenly, her shoes popped off and flames shot out of her pinkie toenails!

FLAMES SHOT OUT OF HER TOENAILS!

(I'm doing it again, aren't I?)

All three of us cried out and leaped back as she kept on sneezing.

"*AH-CHOOO! AH-CHOOO! AH-CHOOO!*"

With every sneeze, the flames shot out farther, until . . .

"AHH . . ." K-WHOOsHHH . . .

her feet zipped off the roof and disappeared into the night. (And since she was connected to her feet, she also zipped off and disappeared into the night.)

"WOW!" I cried. "Did you see that?"

"Some of it," Priscilla said, still wiping her face.

I turned to Splat, who was doing the same with his little paws.

"Was that cool or what?" I cried.

Little did I know that over the next few days the coolness would send cold shivers down my back.

The next morning I woke up to the gentle

screaming of one of my three older sisters.

"BERNIE!"

"Ahh . . ." K-WHOOshhh!

"BERNIE DINGLEDORF, COME DOWN HERE RIGHT NOW!"

I recognized the screaming. But it was the—

"Ahh . . ." K-WHOOshhh!-ing

that had me puzzled.

"BERNIE!"

I hopped out of bed and raced downstairs.

Everybody was standing in the living room. Well, not really standing. More like ducking for cover as . . .

"Ahh . . ." K-WHOOshhh!

"AHH . . ." K-WHOOshhh!

Splat flew back and forth over their heads.

But he was doing more than flying. He was also sneezing.

And, like the B.A.D.D. agent last night, when he sneezed, he sprayed.

"Oh, ick!" Sister 1 screamed.

"He's ruining my hair!" Sister 2 wailed.

"What do we do?" Sister 3 cried.

"Grab an umbrella," Dad spoke quietly. (Dad always speaks quietly—at least compared to my sisters, who always screech *un*quietly.)

"Splat!" I shouted. "What are you doing?"

He couldn't answer. He just kept zooming back and forth over our heads. Zooming, sneezing, and—of course—spraying.

It was definitely raining doggie drool.

In fact, it was so bad that the alarm on my secret agent wristwatch started to sound.

AhoooGaaa . . .
AhoooGaaa . . .

I looked down at it and saw a flashing button that read:

WARNING
PRESS ONLY IF YOU ARE
BEING COVERED IN DOGGIE DROOL

I reached down and pressed it. Suddenly, a giant energy field wrapped around me to protect me. Talk about cool!

But nobody paid any attention. They were all too busy staring up at Splat.

"Look at his toenails!" Sister 1 shouted. "They're on fire!"

But they weren't on fire. Not really. I mean, flames were shooting out of them, but his claws weren't burning up.

It was like the B.A.D.D. agent last night. Splat's toenails weren't on fire. They'd just become rocket-powered. And each time the power started to die down, he would sneeze and they would fire up again.

Oh, and one other thing. Splat's face. It was also glowing green, just like the B.A.D.D. agent's!

"AHH . . ." K-WHOOshhh!

"Bernie," Mom cried, "do you know what's going on?"

I shook my head. "No, Mom."

"He was fine last night," she said. "But this morning, look at him."

"AHH . . ." K-WHOOsHHH!
"AHH . . ." K-WHOOsHHH!

"Did you do anything last night?" she shouted over the roaring and spraying. "Did you go out when you shouldn't?"

And here it came . . .

The thing I shouldn't do . . .

The thing I didn't want to do . . .

The thing I did do . . .

The Lie

"No, Mom."

It was only two words. But two words that would nearly destroy the world.

"Are you sure?" she asked.

"Yes, Mom, I'm sure."

All right, that was four words. I guess
I better start being truthful . . . now.
Too bad I wasn't truthful then.

CHAPTER 2

The Lie Spreads

Later that morning, Priscilla and I headed for school.

"So did you ever catch Splat?" she asked.

"Yeah," I said. "But it took two tennis rackets and a snow shovel to swat him down."

"Poor puppy. Where is he now?"

"We had to tie him to a stake in our backyard."

I pointed toward my fence. You could just see his head floating over the top of the boards as he zipped, zoomed, and

"Ahh . . ." K-WHOOshhh-ed

at the end of his rope.

"And you think he somehow caught it from that B.A.D.D. agent?" she asked.

"Maybe," I said. "Remember when she sneezed all over us?"

Priscilla nodded. "How come we didn't catch it?" she asked.

"I don't know. But his toenails have rocket flames shooting out of them just like hers."

"Wow."

"And he's sneezing just like her."

"Wow."

"And his face is glowing green just like . . . just like . . ." I looked at Priscilla and slowed to a stop.

"What's wrong?" she asked.

"Your face," I said. "It's glowing green!"

She tried covering her cheeks with her hand. "Oh, that," she said. "It's just, uh, uh, it's my new soap. It's called, uh . . . Irish Green!"

I knew she was lying. But before I could ask her about it we heard:

"Hey (*sniff*), guys."

We looked up to see I.Q. joining us. He's supersmart. He's also super (*sniff, sniff*) allergic. And with the smarts and allergies comes—

"Look out!"

K-trip
K-THUD

superclumsiness.

(I don't want to say he has no coordination, but that sound you just heard? It was him falling over his shadow.)

As we helped him to his feet, he pointed at Priscilla's shoes. "What's with those?" he asked.

I looked down and saw she was wearing shoes about fifteen sizes too big.

"They're my older brother's," she said. "Mine wouldn't fit."

"Why not?"

"When I woke up, my pinkie toenails had grown huge."

"Your toenails?" I asked.

"Yeah. And one other thing," she said.

"What's that?"

"I keep having this urge to—"

"AHHH . . . AHHH . . . AHHH . . ."

She shoved her finger under her nose. "To sneeze?" I asked.

She nodded.

"Priscilla!" I cried. "You're turning green and growing big toenails, just like Splat. Just like that secret agent."

"Weird, huh?"

"And now you're about to sneeze. You know what happened when Splat and that agent sneezed!"

"I know," Priscilla said. "But if I keep my finger under my nose, I'll be okay."

"But—"

"You don't want people to connect me and Splat to that agent on your roof last night, do you?"

"Why not?"

"Because then your folks will know you lied about us being up there."

"Yeah, but—"

"You don't want that, do you?"

"No, but—"

"Then we'll have to keep telling every-body I'm okay."

"Yeah, but—"

She gave me a look. "Yeah, but what, Bernie?"

"But it's another lie."

She nodded. "I know, but we have to tell this lie to cover up the first one."

"Yeah, but—"

"But what?!" she demanded.

I looked at her and shrugged. I was running out of "bats." I didn't want to tell another lie, but it looked like we had to in order to cover up the first lie.

Unfortunately, it wouldn't be the last—not by a long shot.

For a while, the lying worked . . .

It worked through morning recess. Each time Priscilla started to

"Ahhh . . . Ahhh . . . Ahhh . . . ,"

she just shoved her finger under her nose and stopped.

No one asked her any questions.

Well, no one but some dorky first grader.

"Hey, girl?" the kid asked. "How come you got your finger under your nose all the time?"

"It's the heat," Priscilla said.

"The heat?"

"Yeah. In this heat, you have to keep your finger under your nose to hold it up. If you don't, it will slide right off your face."

The kid's mouth dropped open. "No way," he said.

"Fine, don't believe me," she said as she turned and walked off.

I stuck my finger under my nose and followed.

He grabbed my arm. "Is that true? What she said?"

"If I were you, I wouldn't take any chances," I said. Then I leaned a little closer and stared. "In fact, it looks like yours is already starting to slip."

He let out a scream and raced off. (First graders, they'll believe anything.)

The lie kept working.

Even in Mrs. Hooplesnort's fourth-grade class.

For a while.

Until . . .

"Priscilla?" Mrs. Hooplesnort asked. "Would you help me carry these books across the room to that other bookshelf?"

"No problem," Priscilla said.

And she was right. It was no problem, except when her arms were completely loaded down with books and she started to

"AHHH . . . AHHH . . . AHHH . . ."

I saw the problem and leaped from my desk. I raced to her and shoved my finger under her nose. It was close, but I made it.

"Thanks," she whispered.

"You going to be okay?" I asked.

She nodded.

"You sure?"

She nodded again.

Slowly, I removed my finger.

She smiled and . . .

"AH-CHOOO!"-ed.

Our eyes both shot down to her feet. Sure enough, flames had already started

burning through the sides of her shoes.

"AH-CHOOO! AH-CHOOO!"

The flames grew longer . . .

"AH-CHOOO! AH-CHOOO! AH-CHOOO!"

and longer and longer, until finally . . .

"*A*HH . . ." K-WHOO*s*HHH!

her feet shot up into the air and she started
zipping around the classroom.

"*A*HH . . ." K-WHOO*s*HHH!
"*A*HH . . ." K-WHOO*s*HHH!
"*A*HH . . ." K-WHOO*s*HHH!

CHAPTER 3

Up, Up, and Awaaaayyy . . .

All of the kids leaped for cover as Priscilla

"*Aʜʜ . . .*" *K-WHOOsʜʜʜ-ed*

around the classroom like some jet fighter.

Well, not exactly like some jet fighter.

Because jet fighters don't have to worry about

K-rash-ing

into overhead lights or . . .

K-bounce K-bounce K-bounc-ing

off classroom walls.

Most important, they don't have to worry about their jet-powered toenails

"Aʜʜ . . ." K-WHOOsʜʜʜ!
sizzle-sizzle-sizzle

lighting Mrs. Hooplesnort's hair on fire.

Actually, it wasn't really her hair. It was just . . .

"My wig!" she cried. "You've set my wig on fire!"

Now, you really can't blame Priscilla and me.

Well, all right, maybe you can blame us. At least about the lying.

But you can't blame us about Mrs.

Hooplesnort's wig. No one even knew she wore one.

And she didn't. Not anymore.

- Not when she ripped it off her head and threw the burning thing onto the floor.

- Not when she did a little tap dance on top of it, trying to put out the flames.

- Not when she had to keep ducking Priscilla's

"AHH . . ." K-WHOOsHHH-ing!

overhead.

Yes sir, it was quite a little show.

It got even better when Priscilla's flaming pinkies finally turned on the

K-SWIIIIIIISHHHH

fire sprinklers, which turned on the

RRRRRRRRRRRRRRRing

fire alarm.

"All right, class!" Mrs. Hooplesnort screamed. "Everybody outside!"

We all obeyed, except for Priscilla. She just kept on

"AHH . . ." K-WHOOSHHH-ing!

as the sprinklers just kept on

K-SWIIIIIIISHHHH-ing

as the fire alarm just kept on

RRRRRRRRRRRRRRRing-ing.

Call it a lucky guess, but I figured Priscilla's little secret was finally out.

Speaking of out, there was one last sound effect I didn't mention. It's the sound someone with rocket-powered toenails makes when they finally

K-RASH
tinkle, tinkle, tinkle

out through a classroom window.

So there we were, out on the playground with the rest of the school.

By now, the entire first-grade class

was holding their fingers under their noses. (I guess the news of sliding noses traveled fast.) Everyone was looking up at Priscilla as she zoomed around, spraying all of us with her

"AHH . . ." K-WHOOsHHH-ing!

"Come down here, young lady!" Principal Lecture started shouting at her. "Come down here this instant!"

beep-beep-beep-beep

He looked around and asked, "What's that noise?"

I recognized the sound. It was my secret agent telephone. The fact that it was also in my secret agent underwear made things a bit more embarrassing.

I pretended not to notice.

beep-beep-beep-beep

He turned to me. "Son . . . are those your underpants ringing?"

Before I could explain, Priscilla zoomed over our heads and . . .

"Aʜʜ . . ." K-WHOOsʜʜʜ
sprinkle, splatter, spray-ed

him good, right in the face with a
sneeze.

"Augh!" he cried as he grabbed a
handkerchief and wiped his face.

This gave me a chance to race behind

the building and yell into my underwear: "Hello?"

"Secret Agent Dingledorf?" It was Big Guy. He was a good agent from the good side. Unfortunately, he also thought I was a secret agent. In fact, he's the one who gave me all the cool secret agent gizmos . . . like my cellular underwear.

"We've got amazing news, Dingledorf."

"You've figured out I'm not a secret agent?" I asked.

"Don't be funny, of course you are an agent," he said. "The world has been exposed to a terrible head cold. It makes people's faces glow green, and they start sneezing, and—"

"Their toenails become jet-powered?" I asked.

"How did you know?"

"A lucky guess," I said. "Where did it come from?"

"There was a B.A.D.D. experiment that went wrong. One of their agents was exposed to it. But she lied and said she wasn't. She spread the cold to somebody else who is now spreading it to others."

I glanced over to Priscilla. Somehow I knew who that somebody else was.

"Did this agent wear a trench coat?" I asked. "Did she have binoculars and a hat, all with the letters B.A.D.D. written on them?"

"Yes! How did you know?"

"Another lucky guess."

"You didn't have anything to do with this, did you?"

I didn't want to lie again. It seemed like the more lies I told, the more I had to keep telling. But I didn't want to get in any more trouble, so I said:

"No, sir."

"Are you sure?"

"Um, well, uh. . . ." I changed subjects. "How come some people catch this cold and others don't?"

"Your name has to begin with the letter *P*."

I nodded and looked up at *P*riscilla. "But what about my dog, Splat?" I asked.

"He has it?"

"Yes. And his name doesn't begin with *P*."

"It doesn't have to be your name. It can also be who or what you are."

"But Splat is a dog. '*Dog*' doesn't begin with *P*."

"Correct. But he's also your pooch," he said. "And '*pooch*' begins with the letter—"

"*P*," I said.

"That's right."

"So why did you call me?" I asked.

"Because we placed a special button in your—"

zap-crackle-hissss-pop

I looked up and saw Priscilla spraying us more than ever with her

"A<small>HH</small> . . ." K-WH00<small>S</small><small>HHH</small>-ing.

"I'm sorry," I shouted into my underpants. "All the wetness from the sneezing is shorting out the phone. Can you repeat?"

"I said, we placed a special button in your watch that will—"

pop-hissss-crackle-zap

"Hello?" I shouted. "Can you hear me? Hello??"

But that was it. My underpants had shorted out.

Things were getting worse. I didn't know what to do or where to go.

But one thing I did know . . . our lying was catching up with us. Big time. Oh, and I knew something else.

"AHH . . ." K-WHOOsHHH

I couldn't wait to get home and change into some dry clothes.

CHAPTER 4

The Lie Keeps Going
and Going and . . .

The next morning, things didn't get a little worse.

THEY GOT A LOT WORSE!

(Sorry, I'm yelling again, aren't I?)

First, there was Mom.

Like Splat, she'd also grown rocket-powered toenails.

When I came into the kitchen she was zipping around overhead.

"Hi, sweetheart—"

"Ahh . . ." K-WHOOshhh

"Got your bacon and eggs right here," she said as she

"Ahh . . ." K-WHOOshhh
K-plink

"Ahh . . ." K-WHOOshhh
K-plop

dropped them onto my plate.
Then there was Dad . . .
"I'm late for work," he said as he

"Ahh . . ." K-WHOOshhh-ed

across the kitchen and gave Mom a kiss before . . .

"A<small>HH</small> . . ." K-WH00<small>S</small>H<small>HH</small>-ing

for the door.

"Mom! Dad!" I cried. "What's going on?!"

"We don't know, sweetheart," Mom said as she shot over my head and tried pouring some milk into my glass.

k-splash, k-splatter,
K-MESS
(Okay, so she's not such a good
shot with the milk.)

"We just woke up this morning with these green faces and these rocket-powered toenails," she explained.

"Just like Splat," Dad added.

"But it only happens to people whose names start with *P!*" I cried.

"How do you know that?"

"Just a lucky guess." (Which, of course, was just another lie.)

"Well," Dad said suspiciously, "we are your

"Aʜʜ . . ." K-WHOOsʜʜʜ-ed

parents."

"Do you know anything about this?" Mom asked me.

Once again, I had the chance to tell the truth. And once again I, um, well, you know, kinda . . . didn't.

"No," I said.

Mom stared at me a moment.

Dad stared at me a moment.

If there had been anybody else there, they'd have probably stared at me a moment, too.

Talk about feeling guilty.

Unfortunately, I still didn't feel guilty enough to tell the truth.

Finally, Dad opened the door and started for the car. "Well, look at this," he shouted from the porch.

I followed him outside.

It was terrible. Not only were everybody's *p*arents flying around, but so were their *p*ets!

I'm not kidding. Everything from

"Aнн . . ." K-WHOOsнн

yap-yap-yap

*p*oodles to

"Aнн . . ." K-WHOOsннн

tweet-tweet-tweet

*p*arakeets to

"AHH . . ." K-WHOOshhh

"Ouch! Ouch! Ouch!"

a *p*orcupine that folks fed at the nearby park.

"Somebody's got to do something!" I cried.

"I don't know what," Dad said. "Nobody knows what's causing it."

I felt terrible. I felt awful.

But I still didn't feel like telling the truth.

Instead, I raced inside and called 9-1-1.

When they answered, I could barely hear. There was too much noise in the background.

"Hello!" I shouted. "Hello, can you hear me?"

"I'm sorry," the voice shouted. "You'll have to speak up."

I shouted as loud as I could. "We need a bunch of ambulances in our neighborhood right away!"

"What?"

"WE NEED AMBULANCES!"

"I'm sorry, but none of our paramedics can help!"

"WHAT?"

The voice repeated, "I said, none of our paramedics can help! They're all busy flying around the—

"AHH . . ." K-WHOOsHHH
"AHH . . ." K-WHOOsHHH
"AHH . . ." K-WHOOsHHH

hospital."

I rubbed my head. Of course, . . . *p*ara-medics.

"WHAT ABOUT THE DOCTORS?" I shouted.

"I'm sorry," the voice yelled. "The same goes for all of our

"*Aнн . . .*" K-WHOOsннн
"*Aнн . . .*" K-WHOOsннн
"*Aнн . . .*" K-WHOOsннн

*p*hysicians."

I closed my eyes. Things kept getting worse and worse. Then I heard it. Outside our house. The sound of a police siren.

Great, someone had called the police. Maybe they could put an end to all of this craziness.

I raced for the door.

"Don't forget your lunch," Mom called.

I grabbed the lunch bag and headed outside.

A police car rounded the corner and zoomed toward us.

Good thing, too. Because the air wasn't just full of flying *p*arents and *p*ets. It looked like the head cold had spread to animals at our local zoo.

That's right. Now there were also *p*eacocks, *p*enguins, and

"Ahh . . ." K-WHOOshhh
"ROARRRRR . . ."

one flying *p*olar bear.

The police car screeched to a stop and the doors swung open.

Now we would be safe.

Now things would be under control.

Now things would be worse than ever!

Because as soon as they stepped out of their car, the *p*olice immediately began

"Ahh . . ." K-WHOOshhh
"Ahh . . ." K-WHOOshhh

sneezing and flying!

CHAPTER 5

Follow the Bouncing Dingledorf

"**A**gent Dingledorf! Agent Dingledorf!"

I looked up and saw one of the flying penguins. At least that's what I thought it was. But there was something about the way the letters B.A.D.D. were printed on its tail feathers . . . and across its wings . . . and on its white belly that made me a little suspicious.

(Then there was the fact that it was calling out my name. That made me *a lot* suspicious.)

"Hey," I shouted. "You're not really a penguin!"

"Of course not, this is just a disguise,"

he yelled. "Though it is making me a little hungry for fish."

"What do you want?" I cried.

"Have you seen our B.A.D.D. agent?" he asked as he fluffed and cleaned his feathers. "We think she's responsible for spreading all these head colds. Her last known location was in your tree spying on you."

Finally. Here was my chance to tell the truth and come clean.

Unfortunately, Mom and Dad were

"AHH . . ." K-WHOOsHHH-ing

nearby, so it was also my chance to continue lying.

I opened my mouth. Before I could stop myself, I said, "Nope, no sir, huh-uh, no way, absolutely not, I don't know what on earth you're talking about."

(Not only was I lying more, I was lying longer.)

He flew closer. "But we've got pictures of you." He pecked at my arm.

"Ow!" I started backing up.

"We've got videotape of you." Another peck on the other arm.

"Ow!"

"We've got—" He stopped and gave a sniff. "Is that a tuna fish sandwich in your lunch bag?"

I figured now was the time to take a stand.

Now was the time to be brave and courageous.

Now was the time to run like the wind!!!

I turned and raced down the street.

"After him!"

I looked over my shoulder. Now, a whole herd of penguins was flying after me.

(Do penguins fly in herds? Do penguins even fly?)

I didn't know, and I wasn't stopping to ask.

Faster and faster I ran.

Closer and closer

"AHH . . ." K-WHOOsHHH
"AHH . . ." K-WHOOsHHH

they came.

Suddenly, the alarm on my secret agent watch started to sound.

AhoooGaaa . . .
AhoooGaaa . . .

I looked down at it. Another one of the buttons was glowing. On it were the flashing words:

WARNING
PRESS ONLY IF ATTACKED
BY A HERD OF PENGUINS

With nothing else better to do (but save my life), I reached for the button.

Unfortunately, it was about this time that my bird buddy pecked at my hand, causing my finger to slip and hit the wrong button.

No problem. With so many buttons to choose from, I figured it didn't make that much difference.

And it didn't. Well, except for the part where my shirt sleeves and pant cuffs suddenly

K-lamp, K-lamp
K-lamp, K-lamp-ed

down around my wrists and ankles.

Then there was the little matter of my clothes, which suddenly

K-PLOOOOF

filled up with air.

We're not talking a little amount of air, here. We're talking hot-air-balloon amount of air. In fact, you couldn't even see my arms and legs sticking out. It's like I'd become one giant ball.

And with no more arms or legs, there was no more running. Now there was only . . .

roll-roll-roll-roll-ing

and a lot of

bounce-bounce-bounc-ing

So there I was, Bernie the human soccer ball, rolling and bouncing down the street.

To be honest, once I got the hang of it, it was kind of cool. With all that air around me, I was so padded that I couldn't get hurt. All I could do was . . .

HONK! HONK! HONK!

get hit by that semitruck coming straight
at me.

SEMITRUCK COMING
STRAIGHT AT ME!!

(All right, all right, this time I am yelling. But for good reason.

Have you ever seen what a semitruck can do to a soccer ball?)

CHAPTER 6

Splat to the Rescue . . .
Well, Sort Of

So there I was, bouncing down the street like some giant soccer ball.

Even that wasn't so bad, except for the soccer players. . . .

On one team was my friend, the giant semitruck.

HONK! HONK! HONK!
K-Thunk! K-Bop! K-Pow!

(In case you're wondering,

that's the sound human

soccer balls make when kicked

by giant semitrucks.)

On the other team, coming from the oppo-
site direction, was some little Volkswagen
Beetle

beep-beep

beep-beep

(Hey, he may be little, but he could
still . . .

k-tink! k-tank! k-tunk!

"OW!"

kick.)

And so, the soccer game continued as
they kicked me up and down the street.

K-Thunk! k-tink!

Then down and up the street.

*k-tink! **K-Thunk!***

What an incredible match they were playing!

What incredible kicks they were making!

What an incredible headache I was getting!

Then, ol' semitruck found an opening and . . .

HONK! HONK!
K-POW!-ed

me high into the air.

I tell you, it was a great view up there.

And it was fun visiting all my friends and relatives with the jet-powered toenails.

"Hey, Mom."

"Hello—"

"Ahh . . ." K-WHOOshhh

"sweetheart."

"How's it going, Priscilla?"

"Not—

"*Ahh . . .*" *K-WHOOshhh*

bad. But stay away from the polar bear. He's kind of cranky."

Unfortunately, what goes up (even if it's a human soccer ball) must come

"AUGH!"
K-THUD

down.

The good news was, *down* meant down into my own backyard.

The bad news was, Splat

"Woof! Woof!"

was still tied up there. Well, he *had* been tied up there.

He got so excited seeing me, he broke free and leaped on top of me.

No problem, except for his sharp little claws.

"No, Splat! Stay down! Down, boy!"

His sharp little claws that dug into my balloon clothing, which suddenly went

sssssssssssssssssssss
K-POP
PSSSSSSSSSss ss s

Once again I was flying. Only this time I had a copilot. Yes sir, Splat clung to me tighter than those ugly hiphugger jeans on my sisters.

Together, we zipped all over the place.

Unfortunately, "all over the place" also included straight toward the overhead power lines.

OVERHEAD POWER LINES!

(There I go again.)

Suddenly, another alarm on my watch went off.

I looked down and saw another flashing button. This one read:

WARNING
PRESS ONLY IF YOU ARE
ABOUT TO HIT POWER LINES

Having no desire to wind up like a bug in one of those bug zappers (are those things gross, or what?), I reached down, pressed the button, and . . .

we were no longer going to hit the power lines.

The reason was simple. We were no longer going to hit the power lines because we'd been turned into electricity. Now we were going *inside* the power lines!

(Don't you just hate it when that happens?)

Great, I thought. *Now what?*

Unfortunately, I was about to find out.

CHAPTER 7

Invading Pickles

The cool thing about being electricity is you get to shoot through wires at a gazillion miles an hour.

The bad thing about being electricity is those wires have to end somewhere. For Splat and me that somewhere was

KLUNK

inside somebody's computer.

But not just anybody's computer. No, that would have been too normal. (And as we all know, these cases are anything but normal.)

Instead, when Splat and I looked out from inside the monitor, we saw . . . the B.A.D.D. secret agent who had started it all.

THE B.A.D.D. SECRET AGENT WHO HAD STARTED IT ALL!

(Sorry.)

That's right. She was sitting in front of the screen. And though her face was still green and she kept on

"*AH-CHOOO!*"-ing,

she didn't fly all over the room. The reason was simple. She had tied herself down into a chair.

"Hey!" she shouted. "What are you two doing inside my video game?"

"Video game?" I yelled.

"Yeah! My Space Invader video game!"

Before I could answer, I heard:

"GIVE IT UP, EARTHLING. YOU
ARE SURROUNDED."

I turned just in time to see a computer character, which looked like a giant *p*ickle, fire his

squirt—zap

laser pickle gun at me.

I wasn't worried. After all, he was only a computer character.

The only problem was,

squirt-zap "Ouch!"

so was I. And so was

squirt-zap "Woof!"

Splat.

That's right. We'd both been shot. And by the way our rears were smoking from the pickle-juice lasers, we both knew where.

Suddenly, I heard my

beep-beep-beep-beep

underwear ringing.

I lowered my head and shouted, "Hello?"

"Agent Dingledorf?"

"Big Guy?" I cried. "What's going on?!"

He answered. "We programmed your watch to track down the B.A.D.D. agent."

"Why?" I shouted.

"You must convince her to tell the truth. She must admit that she was exposed to the head cold. And she must turn herself in so we can find a cure."

"But—"

"There's no other way to stop the flying toenails."

"But—"

"Hurry!" Big Guy shouted. "There isn't much time."

I nodded. "You're telling—

squirt-zap "Ouch!"

me!"

I'd barely hung up before the B.A.D.D. agent shouted, "Will you guys get out of that game?! You're ruining my score!"

"We've been sent to tell you to stop lying!" I cried. "You have to turn yourself in and tell the truth!"

"Me?" she shouted. "What about you?"

"What about me?"

"I've been watching you on my remote monitors. You haven't exactly been telling the truth."

"Yeah, but . . ."

"But what?"

"Well, my lies aren't as big as your lies!"

"Oh yeah?" she said.

"Yeah!" I said.

"Yeah??" she said.

"Yeah!!" I said.

"Yeah???" she said.

"Yeah!!!" I—(Well, you probably get the picture.)

The point is, we weren't so great at arguing.

Unfortunately, we were a lot better at fighting. Well, at least she was.

"Take this!" she shouted. She pressed a button on her remote control and

rrrRRRRrrrRRRRrrrRRRR . . .

forty computer game spaceships landed around us.

No problem.

Then forty doors zipped open on those forty spaceships.

zip zip zip zip zip zip zip zip zip zip
zip zip zip zip zip zip zip zip zip zip
zip zip zip zip zip zip zip zip zip zip
zip zip zip zip zip zip zip zip zip zip

Still, no problem.

Then about 100 million invading space pickles rolled out of those forty doors.

Okay, now we had a problem.

Oh, yeah, and they all squirted their 100 million laser pickle guns at us.

squirt-zap "Ouch!"
squirt-zap "Ouch!"
(Don't make me write 100 million of these, okay? Thanks.)

Yes sir, we were definitely toast.

squirt-zap "Ouch!"
(Make that *burnt* toast.)

Then, all of a sudden, the pickles started sneezing.

And when they sneezed, their toenails fired up and they started

"AHH . . ." K-WHOOsHHH-ing

all around the video screen.

"You're ruining my game!" the B.A.D.D. agent cried. "You're ruining my game!"

"It's not us!" I shouted. "It's the head cold! It attacks anybody whose name begins with the letter *P!*"

"But they're space invaders!" she cried. "They don't have names."

"AHH . . ." K-WHOOShHH
"AHH . . ." K-WHOOShHH

"I know," I shouted. "But what type of space invaders are they?"

"Well, they're green and tall and bumpy and—"

"They're *p*ickles!" I shouted. "They're space invading *p*ickles!"

"So?"

"So how do pickles begin?"

"Well, they start off as cucumbers, then you soak them in—"

"No!" I shouted. "What *letter* do they begin with?"

(I tell you, for a secret agent, she wasn't the brightest candle on the cake.)

Finally, she got it.

"Oh, no!" she shouted. "The letter *P!* *P*ickles begin with the letter *P!*"

CHAPTER 8

The Case Closes

"What do we do?" the B.A.D.D. agent cried. "My video game is being destroyed!"

"Not to mention the world!" I said. "But you can stop it!"

"How?"

"Admit how you caught your cold. Turn yourself in and tell the truth!"

"What about you?" she said.

"My lie was smaller."

"Maybe in the beginning. But take a look now."

She hit a couple of keys on her keyboard. Suddenly, the screen lit up with all the parents and pets . . .

"Ahh . . ." K-WHOOshhh-ing

around our city.

"Yeah," I shouted, "but—"

She hit another key that showed all the *p*eople in our state with the virus

"Ahh . . ." K-WHOOshhh-ing

"Yeah, but—"

Then another key, and our country, even our beloved *p*resident and all the *p*oliticians, were sneezing and flying around.

It was awful. Worse than awful! And I knew I was partly to blame!

"All right!" I shouted. "All right! If you turn yourself in, I'll tell the truth!"

"Are you sure?" she asked.

"Yes!" I cried.

"Do you promise?"

"Yes, I promise, I promise!"

"Let's shake on it," she said.

"All right!"

I reached my hand up to the computer screen.

She reached her hand down to the computer screen.

And then, just before we touched . . .

"AHH . . ." K-WHOOsHHH

she let loose the wettest sneeze of all.

It covered the keyboard with so much spray that

K-rackle, hiss, pop,
and K-rackle some more

it shorted out the entire computer. Everything went blank.

"Hello?" I shouted.

No answer.

"Hello?"

Repeat in the No-Answer Department.

But I wasn't too worried. I knew she'd tell the authorities and get me out. Because even though she was a B.A.D.D. agent, she knew there were some things badder than B.A.D.D.

Like me, she'd seen all the damage lying can do. And I knew she'd tell the truth.

Just as important, I knew I would.

By the end of the week, things had started to settle down.

The B.A.D.D. agent turned herself in and told the truth about being exposed to the head cold.

I told the truth about being on the roof and getting Splat and Priscilla exposed (along with the rest of the world).

Soon the doctors were able to find a cure and start giving everybody shots. Well, everybody who had the virus.

"Did the shot hurt?" I asked Priscilla as we headed across the playground.

"Not as much as our lying," she said.

"I know what you mean," I agreed. "Telling lies can really stink."

Priscilla nodded. "Even the little ones."

She was right. A lie is a lie. Whether it's big or small, fat or skinny, black or white, it's all the same. A lie is a lie.

"Bernie . . ."

I looked up to see the dorky first grader running toward us.

"How come you guys aren't holding your fingers under your noses?" he asked.

"Because it's silly," Priscilla said.

He frowned and pointed across the playground. The kindergartners, the first graders, even the second graders were all running around with their fingers under their noses.

"It may be silly," he said, "but nobody's lost a nose, yet."

Priscilla and I looked at each other.

"That's not the problem anymore," Priscilla said.

"It isn't?" he asked.

She shook her head. Then she reached up and stuck her fingers in her ears.

"What are you doing?" he said.

"What?" she yelled.

"I said, what are you doing?"

"I'm holding my brains in. With all this heat it's the only way to stop them from running out!"

"What?"

She nodded.

"No way!" he cried.

She shrugged. "If you want to take the chance, go ahead." With that, she turned and walked off.

He looked to me with his eyes big and frightened. "She's not telling the truth, is she?" he asked.

"Let me get back to you on that," I said.

He nodded and dashed off.

I turned and followed after Priscilla. "Priscilla?" I shouted. "Priscilla?!"

She finally came to a stop and sighed.

"I know, I know . . . but I couldn't resist."

We both turned and watched. Already a couple of the first graders were running around with their fingers in their ears.

"We better tell them the truth," I said.

She nodded. "Yeah, we better."

Suddenly, my underwear started to

beep-beep-beep-beep.

I figured it was Big Guy wanting me to solve another case, probably save the world again. (Either that or it was one of those phone guys trying to sell me something.)

beep-beep-beep-beep

Either way, they'd have to wait. Because right now there were more important things to do. Like going back and being honest with those kids.

Because, even though saving the world is important . . . so is telling the truth.

Look for These Other Books in This Series

The Case of the Giggling Geeks

The world's smartest people can't stop laughing. Is this the work of the crazy criminal Dr. Chuckles? Only Secret Agent Dingledorf (the country's greatest agent, even though he is just ten years old) can find out. Together, with super cool inventions (that always backfire), major mix-ups (that become major mishaps), and the help of Splat the Wonder-dog, our hero winds up saving the day . . . while discovering the importance of respecting and loving others.
ISBN 1-4003-0094-0

www.tommynelson.com

A Division of Thomas Nelson, Inc.
www.ThomasNelson.com

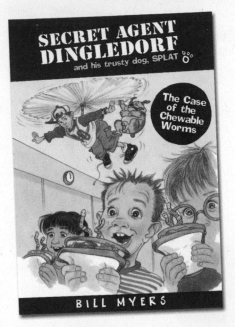

The Case of the Chewable Worms

The earth is being invaded by worms! They're everywhere
. . . crawling on kid's toothbrushes, squirming in their
sandwiches. And worst of all, people find them . . . tasty!
But is it really an invasion or the work of B.A.D.D.
(Bungling Agents Dedicated to Destruction)? Only Secret
Agent Dingledorf and his trusty dog, Splat, can find out
and save the day . . . while also realizing the importance
of doing good and helping others.   ISBN 1-4003-0095-9

www.tommynelson.com

A Division of Thomas Nelson, Inc.
www.ThomasNelson.com